# LOS ANGELES
# RAVE FLYERS
## 1991 - 1994

*For Victor Stapf
of Synthetrix*

FULL FORCE
Truth
EVERY TWO WEEKS
FIRST CLASS
US POSTAGE
PAID
LOS ANGELES CALIF
PERMIT NO 1240

STEVE OF MOONSHINE     THE A.G.N. OF BOOGIE LOUNGE
GIVING THANKS
Truth
saturday
november 30th
at the Park Plaza
607 S. Park View
10pm - 4am
LIVE SHOW
TO BE ANNOUNCED
????
MICHAEL COOK
MARK LEWIS
JOHN WILLIAMS
ALI WOD
OF AFRICAN UNITY
ROB HARRIS
MASTER BEE
PLUS GUESTS
EARLY ARRIVAL RECOMMENDED - INFO 213 550 1947 - 21 W/ID

TRUTH

STEVE OF MOONSHINE    TEF OF LOST ANGELS    A.G.N. OF BOOGIE LOUNGE & THIRST
THE RETURN OF
Truth
NO BULLSHIT!!
10PM - 4AM SATURDAY
NOVEMBER 9TH
AT THE PARK PLAZA
607 S. PARK VIEW
INFO & MAIL LIST: 213 550 1947
ARRIVE EARLY TO AVOID THE LINE! — 21 W/ID — COVER ONLY $15!!
MULTIPLIED & MAXIMIZED
4x FULL ROOMS FOR MAXIMUM ENERGY
3x FULL SPECTRUM COLOR LAZERS
MONSTER SOUND SYSTEMS
ORBS OF TRUTH BY XFX
2x ROOMS TO RAVE TO
THE MASTERS OF THE HOUSE
MARK LEWIS   MICHAEL COOK
DOM T.      JUSTIN KING
1x FUNKED UP
ROB HARRIS
MASTER BEE
REGGAE DJ
ALY WOD OF
AFRICAN UNITY
Fx OPTIKINETICS FROM THE MILKY WAY
PROJECTING THE TRUTH BY XFX
ULTIMATE INTELLABEAM LIGHT WAVE

ULTRA
Truth
BASSLINE FRESH
ROADS
R2H
Truth
SATURDAY JULY 13TH
AND EVERY TWO WEEKS
TRUTH
RIDING THE SUMMER OF LOVE
SATURDAY JULY 27TH
Truth
100% PURE ENERGY
AND EVERY TWO WEEKS
SURPASSING ALL EXPECTATIONS
Truth
BUSTING OUT ON THE SCENE
JUST 1 SCOOP IS ALL IT TAKES
TRUTH
FUNKY RESERGENT
GIVING IT LOADS
Truth
RAVE ON...TRIP OUT
AN OUNCE
Truth
300% PURE FUN
A RAVE TO REMEMBER
NEW AND IMPROVED
FUNKIN' GOOD NEWS
LIVE SHOW BY
DOUBLE FREAK
TRUTH
EVEN MORE INGREDIENTS
SATISFIES ALL REQUIREMENTS
THE WHOLE
AND NOTHING BUT

GLOBAL
NASA
PROJECT
Bold
B
B
B
WAVE OF THE FUTURE
no guts
no glory
100% BUST FREE
WAREHOUSE
coming
SATURDAY
MAY 22, 1999

NASA

Bold

THE WAVE OF THE FUTURE
EXPEDITIONARY SPACE GUIDES
ROCKY RACKOON & HOUSE OF FIERCE RULING DIVAS

(213) 969.1316
LAUNCH INFORMATION
(213) 955.5252

(714) 665.7799
LAUNCH INFORMATION
(310) 804.8791

LEADING YOU INTO A CLOSE ENCOUNTER
OF THE 5TH KIND WITH D.J.'S
MR. KOOL-AID
BARRY WEAVER
LENNY V
MR. FLASHBACK
SUPER SPACE BASS
JBL CONCERT SERIES SOUND
SHREDDER

INTELLIGENT INTELLIBEAMS IN FULL FX
E-LO • TECHNOCOLOR
AMAZE YOUR HUMAN VISION
AS GO-GO DANCERS TRANSPORT
YOU TO ANOTHER GALAXY!
COMMUNICATE
WITH PLANET MARS AND BEYOND
WITH LAZERS BY MIRAGE
SUPER SMART BAR • FRESH PRODUCE • CONCESSIONS
RETURN OF THE DAY-GLO HUMAN BODY ART
FUNKY 70'S ROOM WITH THE PIMP DADDY DJ SHAGG E.

FREE SPACE GEAR
candy • lollipops • toys
t-shirts • mixed tapes • whistles

MDM DESIGN 937.1031

CYBER
CIRCUS
FRI.
1992

EVAR PRODUCTIONS & S.P.R.K.TRONIC
UNITE ALL OF SOUTHERN CALIF. WITH
CYBER CIRCUS
FRIDAY JUNE 26, 1992
WITH YOUR CYBER ACTIVATED HOSTS: PAUL, BRIAN OF
SKIN TWO> BRANDON, NICK - OPIUM> DAVEN THE MAD HATTER>
BEEJ/BLITZ> MIKE HIATUS - CLOBBER>
LES OF TECHNOFLIGHT> STATIK LINE>
LIVE AND DIRECT ON
STAGE, PERFORMING
100% DIGITAL>
DIMENSION 23
...FEATURING JEWELL EE...
BLEU
...ZOO RAVE COMPILATION...
POSITRONIC RINGMASTERS
DALE CHARLES
MR. KOOL AID
JON BISHOP
MARKEM'X
X STATIC
70'S
CYBERDELIC GROOVE LOUNGE
SEAN "BIG
DADDY" PERRY
INTERACTIVE FRACTALS/LAZERS STIMULATION E-LUMMINATED
SPECIAL FX AND LIGHTING ILLUSIONS CAT IN THE HAT
COMPUTER GENERATED SLIDE IMAGERY MIKE HELL
SONIC BOOM SOUND THUNDER HILL
INFO [619] 496-6662 [714] 647-7113 [213] 960-5103
THIS EVENT WILL NOT BE SMALL
FIRE GRAPHIX
479-8616
CUSTOM PRINTING SERVICES

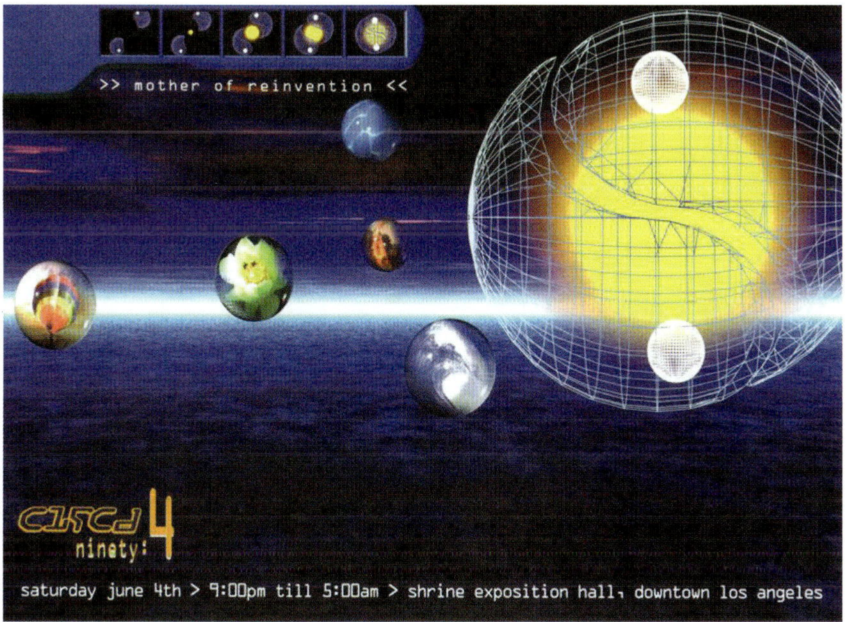

>> mother of reinvention <<
circa
ninety: 4
saturday june 4th > 9:00pm till 5:00am > shrine exposition hall, downtown los angeles

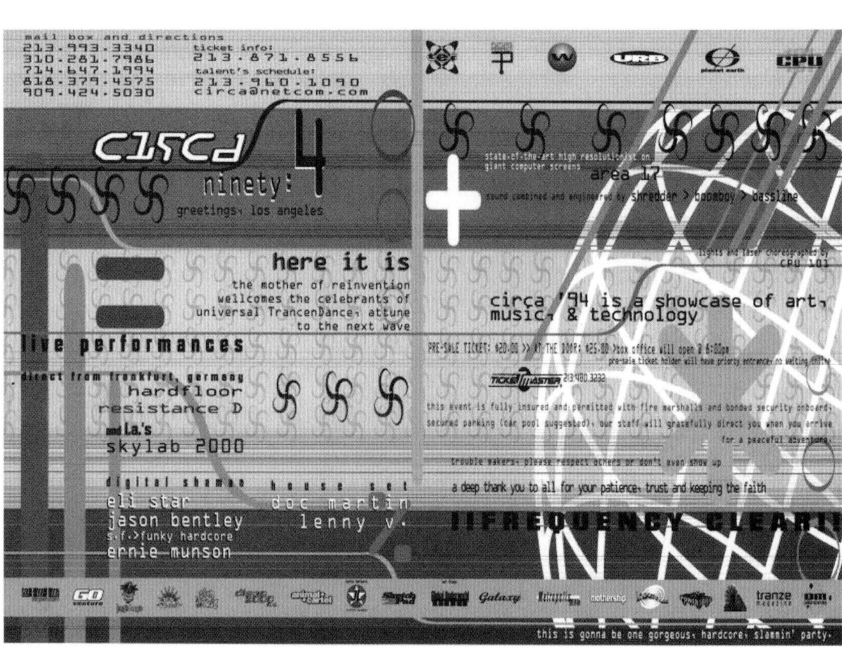

mail box and directions
213.993.3340
310.281.7986
714.647.1994
818.379.4575
909.424.5030
ticket info:
213.871.8556
talent's schedule:
213.960.1090
circa@netcom.com
circa 4
ninety: 4
greetings, los angeles
here it is
the mother of reinvention
wellcomes the celebrants of
universal TrancenDance, attune
to the next wave
live performances
direct from frankfurt, germany
hardfloor
resistance D
and l.a.'s
skylab 2000
digital shaman
eli star
jason bentley
s.f.->funky hardcore
ernie munson
house set
doc martin
lenny v.
state-of-the-art high resolution art on
giant computer screens
area 17
sound combined and engineered by shredder > boomboy > bassline
lights and laser choreographed by
CPU 101
circa '94 is a showcase of art,
music, & technology
PRE-SALE TICKET: $20.00 >> AT THE DOOR: $25.00 >box office will open @ 6:00pm
pre-sale ticket holder will have priorty entrance; no waiting inline
TICKETMASTER 213.480.3232
this event is fully insured and permitted with fire marshalls and bonded security onboard,
secured parking (car pool suggested), our staff will gracefully direct you when you arrive
for a peaceful adventure.
trouble makers, please respect others or don't even show up
a deep thank you to all for your patience, trust and keeping the faith
!!FREQUENCY CLEAR!!
this is gonna be one gorgeous, hardcore, slammin' party.
Galaxy
mothership
tranze
om

saturday
december 19th
come daydream your mind away on...
CLOUD
NINE

big fluffy dj's
CLOUD NINE
CHRIS FLORES
TOM LEWIS
& his hip hoppin' funk
the mac daddy
MR. FLASHBACK
greatest show on earth
JOHNNY AFTERSHOCK
l.a. goes banans
concessions by
"A HAT"   GYRO
DIVA
TRIBAL   JOKE!
DR. SISKO
special guest from
sonics adventures
your hosts
MOOKIE
& GIDGET
bill macing
MDM
937.1031
PROMOTIONAL CONSIDERATION
the sisters   s.o.u.l
tony k.   latin underground
dnm III
special live
hip hop performers
BUDDA VILLE BOYZ
SATURDAY
DEC. 19th
call for weather info!
213
356-1025
310
335-0932

Camp Snoopy
Woodstock 92
JUNE 12,13,14

The WIZARD Presents

Camp Snoopy

JUNE 12, 13, 14

L.A's first 3 day rave
Please bring sleeping bags & tents
for this event will take place in a

FOREST

Providing the pump
Michael Cook        Doc Martin                    Aero
Scott Hardkiss      Barry Weaver  Mike Messex
Jon Williams        Moon Pup          "Big Daddy"
Steve Loria                              SeanPerry

Live Reggae Festival Saturday Afternoon

Providing the ambiant surroundings

Mirage      Shredder       Visual Symphony

Come join us on this full moon weekend
and discover what it really means to rave.

818 502 4224
213 259 3282

raw vibes
U. S. a.
Fresh Jive Mfg. Inc.

WIZARDRY
Productions

Only you
can prevent
forest fires

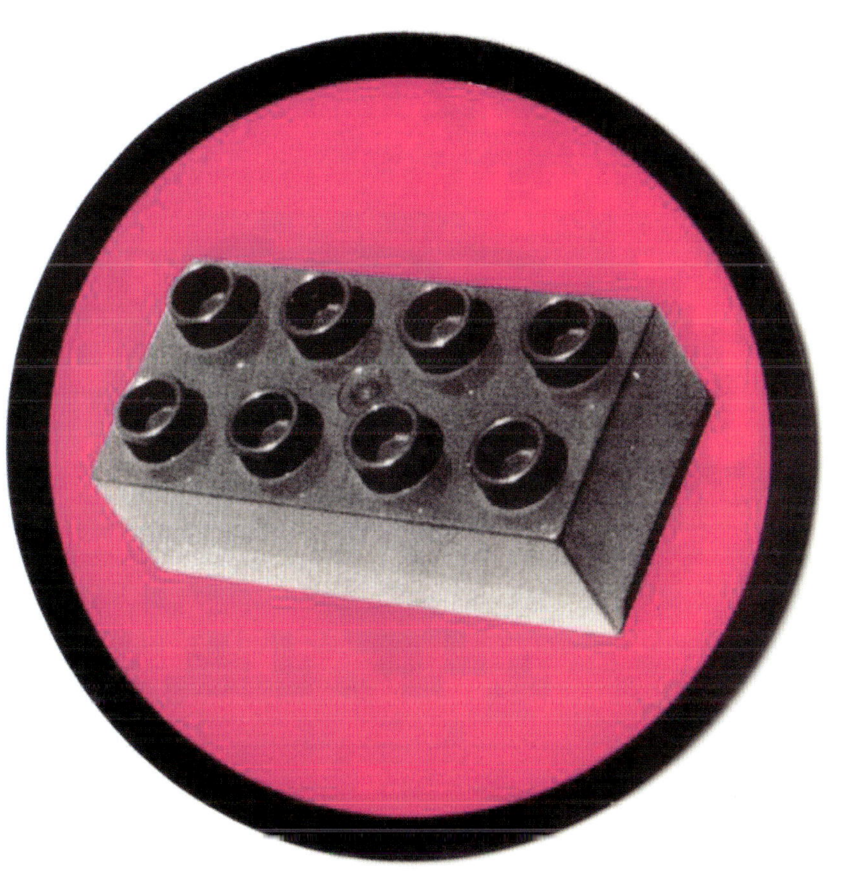

cloBBer™
size
style
price

GRAPE APE
2

# DON'T BE LEFT OUT OF THE JUNGLE ON SAT-SEPT 19, THE EVENT OF 1992 AS NIGHT TURNS TO DAY.

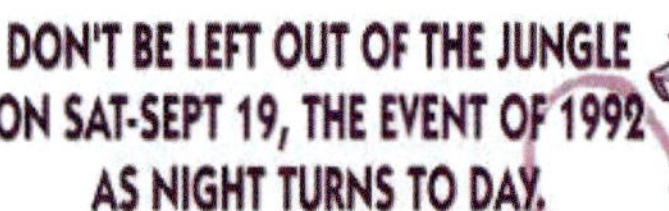


The Vine continues to grow **OUR WORLD OUR FUTURE PRODUCTIONS - CREATORS OF GRAPE APE PRESENT GRAPE APE II** - We Grapefully invite you to thee Original Monkey Around Underground - Take A Safari into The Land of Love and Freedom, Escaping into a realm of complete imagination and creation – **JUNGLE RHYTHMIC** beats layed down by **TRIBAL CHIEFS DJ DAN & RON D CORE (DX-2) W/EXPANDO DOC MARTIN, BARRY WEAVER, R.A.W., E-ZONE, MARK E QUARK** of **SAN DIEGO, FABIAN, ROBIN, DJ MELLINFUNK,** and **DJ DONALD GLAUDE** of **SEATTLE** and **DJ NEON LEON** of **SAN FRANCISCO** laying down the laws in the Tribal Funkroom **DJ RX** and **MILKY** continuing for filling the happiness of Funk and Groove, the inauguration of this event will feature Live Performances by **70's LEGENDS KC & SUNSHINE BAND** with **STRICTLY RHYTHMIC RECORDING ARTISTS POLITIX OF DANCING, DJ DIGIT, DJ EFX** of **SAN FRANCISCO** From **NEW YORK MYX RECORDING ARTIST SCOTT BLACKWELLS DEEP GOSPEL HOUSE**

One Godzillion Watts of Jungle Bass by **SHREDDER** and **BOOM BOY**
Hazy Jungle Lighting by **LECTRA LITE** and **CAT IN THE HAT**
Misty Smooder Optical Projections and visuals by **X-FX BRAD BAKER** and
**AGE OF MACHINES LABRATORYS**
**LIVE STONE AGE THEATRICS** performed by **JIM MARTIN**
Swinging Jungle Aerial Combat Tactics featuring **THE SCREAMING SQUEEGEES SK8 BOARD EXHIBITION TEAM** including **OMAR HASSAN & CHRISTIAN HOSOI** and friends
Live Hieroglyphic painting upon numerous footage of vertical walls by **CBS & SMD** of L.A.
Plus Jungle Toy to fill your joy featuring **FUN JUMP MOON BOUNCE, EDDIE BIG CHAIR, GRAPE APE JUNGLE JAVA AND SMART BAR, SURVIVAL GRAB BAGS,** concessions by **26RED, EUROFUNK HONEST MIKE, SPLATTWEAR, HAPPY CAT, EX-PLOR, MISS KITTY, MICHOACAN JUNGLE BERRY ICE POP VENDORS** and **MANY MORE—**
And The Return of the infamous **FUNKY, STOOPID, FRESH H20 PETS**

Featuring

Guaranteed once again bringing back old school basic positive energy no driving adventures in the land of stress and anxiety
Special Thank Yous to all of our Friends and Family and to all the Ravers who support the scene of style, expression and freedom
## —Thank You and RAVE ON!—

**(714) 647-7163 (213) 960-1082 (714) 55-Noise • SIDE SHOW HOT LINE (714) 399-1836 (415) 266-9217 (619) 597-1437**

ULTRA
Truth
MORE BOUNCE TO THE OUNCE
BASSLINE FRESH
GIVING IT MORE
LOADS
EVERY TWO WEEKS

GEORGE & STEVE FROM MOONSHINE & BORA BORA
TEF FROM LOST ANGELS & PAPA WILLY
THE WEDDING
GIVE YOU MORE OF THE
Truth

SATURDAY
MARCH 9th
10PM - 4AM

AT THE PARK PLAZA
607 S. PARK VIEW
ON THE ULTIMATE
25,000 WATT SOUND SYSTEM

LIVE PERFORMANCE BY
BOYS WONDER
FRESH FROM LONDON

CLEANING THE HOUSE
MARK LEWIS of MOONSHINE
MICHAEL COOK of MR. BUBBLE

IN THE FUNK CYCLE
MIKE MESSEX
D    J    P
SKATEMASTER TATE

PROBING YOUR MIND WITH PROJECTIONS BY BRAD BAKER
NEVER SEEN BEFORE COMPUTER VISUALS BY WARREN KLINE
QUAD INTELLABEAM LIGHTING BY ULTIMATE
EARLY ARRIVAL SUGGESTED
21:ID NO EXCEPTIONS
FURTHER INFO 213-476-6243

FRESH
JIVE

FUNKY RESERGENT
GIVING IT LOADS
Truth
RAVE ON...TRIP OUT
AN OUNCE

GEORGE & STEVE FROM MOON SHINE
TEF FROM LOST ANGELS
THE ARTIST GROOVE NETWORK
FROM THE BOOGIE LOUNGE
UNLEASH THE POWER OF
SATURDAY
JUNE 29TH
AT THE PARK PLAZA
607 S. PARK VIEW
ULTRA Truth
THX SOUND SYSTEM BY CHRIS COMBS
ULTIMATE ITELLABEAM LIGHTING
PROJECTIONS BY XFX & MILKY WAY MIKE
JOURNEY TO CENTER OF YOUR MIND
WITH THREE MUSICAL CYCLES
PRESS E FOR ENERGY WITH
MARK LEWIS
MICHAEL COOK
AND FROM LONDONS WAG
DOM T.
PRESS F FOR FUNK
MIKE MESSEX
ROB HARRIS
BACK WITH LIVE
BACK SPIN
SELETIONS
RAYSKI
RHYTHM POSSE
early arrival encouraged   21w/ID  FUTHER INFO (213) 550 1947
FIRST CLASS
US POSTAGE
PAID
LOS ANGELES,CA
PERMIT NO. 1240

N
OR
MAL

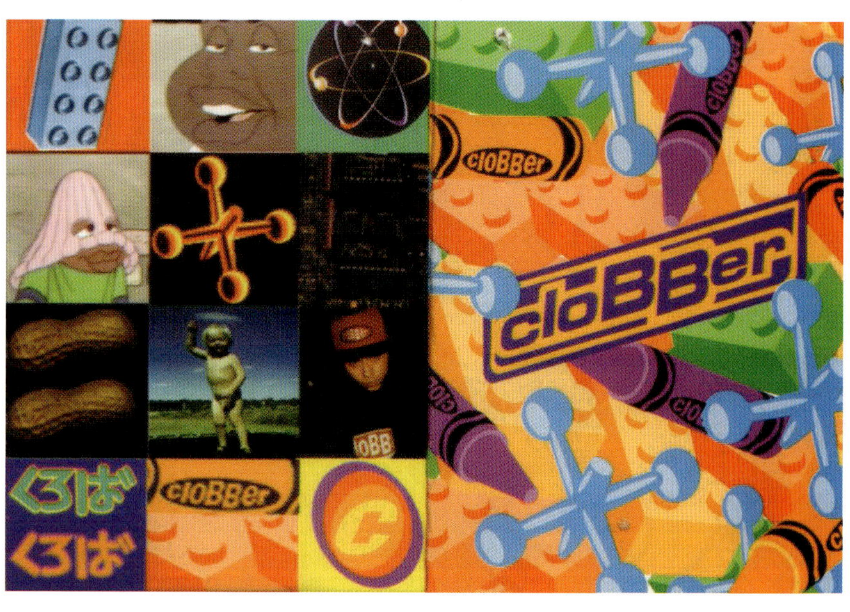

cloBBer
cloBBer
cloBBer
oBB
くろば
くろば
cloBBer

Garden of Eden
Saturday
June 26th, 1993

Trip On This productions presents

# Garden of Eden

trippin dj's

Ron D Core
Dr. Sisko
R.A.W.
Markem'X
Louis Love
benny V.
La Rok

Live Performance to be announced

Sound by
Master Splinter

Behind the Groove
Poisonous Records

trip lines
213.882.4920
310.281.7309
818.556.0105

Saturday
June 26th, 1993

R&R Graphics
214.521.8784

HIGHER LOVE
SATURDAY
August 7, 1993

HIGHER
LOVE
Saturday
August 7, 1993

Barry Weaver
dj's    Lenny V.
Mr. Koolaid
David Alvarado

Loving Vibrations
by
BOOMBOY

Lasers, Lights &
other lovely visuals
Funkin    Cat in the Hat
the Groove
Shag-E    Lovelines
BEEJ    213.960.784 9
818.702.7677

supported by
Family Groove
Shine

brought to u by
Jungle Boogie
& BOSS events

TOTAL HARDCORE ENERGY
Truth
100%
REACTIVATED
RAVE

1992
OASIS
IS HERE AND ONCE MORE WE JOURNEY INTO
SUMMER, AND ONCE AGAIN, TIMES ARE
TOUGHER...WE'RE ON THE MOVE AND ONE
WHO IS ON THE MOVE SHOULD CARRY A GOOD
MAP...THE MAP BY WHICH YOU SHALL
DANCE...YOU'LL NEED QUALITY IN YOUR LIFE,
AND THIS IS WHERE FIT IN.

TRUST OUR EXPERIENCE, AND WE'LL LEAD YOU
TO THE OASIS...DON'T FORGET TO PACK YOUR
BAGS THOUGH...YOU'RE SMART; REMEMBER?

PLANNING IS THE KEY TO OUR SUCCESS,
RECYCLE YOURSELF; PLAY BY THE NEW RULES,
THE FUTURE IS NOT WHAT IT USED TO BE.

THE SUN IS WAITING, THROUGH THE HAZE OF
EXCUSE ME, LET'S KISS THE SKY.

ONCE UPON A TIME, NOT SO LONG AGO
EVERYTHING WAS SIMPLE, WE WERE JUST
STRANDED ON AN ISLAND, NOW IT'S TIME TO
SAIL AWAY...

GILLIGAN'S

live fast
dream hard

MEMORIAL DAY WEEKEND

GILLIGAN
is back with his fearless
gang of L.A. castaways...
LIVE AND DIRECT
VIA CIRCA 92
TEF AND WADE
TAKE YOU TO THE
OTHER SIDE WITH
THE SERMON BOYZ
JAQUES AND GREG
ATOMIC PLAYBOYS- CLIFF AND RICH!!
PLUS! THE FAT DADDY
CREDO PRODUCTIONS
ONCE AGAIN, WE'LL CHANGE
THE STYLE...
SO GET ON BACK WITH
ALL THAT, BUNK HUSTLIN',
NO SHOW, NEVER MIND
THE LAME NAMES.
AND AS ALWAYS... PLEASE,
DON'T BELIVE THE HYPE.
this is the original, we are
the family and this is your world.
We proudly introduce the
future sound of Los Angeles!

OHM

once again prepare yourself for total chaos & unity and lots and lots of fun as we rave and rage in two fun filled rooms of smiling & happy faces as we re-create

the L.A. Riot

$10 bargain secure venue!
you heard right, sunday with no school or work on monday!

GUIDING YOU THROUGH THIS MENTAL MADNESS YOUR RIOT HOST
DJ DESTRUCTO OF DOUBLE HIT MICKEY

LOOTING DJS OUT OF CONTROL CREATING TOTAL CHAOS

RON D. CORE
aphrodite's temple

DJ DAN
quadrophonia

MARKEM X
happy wednesdays

ALDO BENDER
armageddon

straight from the cutting edge
R.A.W.

ALSO INTRODUCING THEE L.A. PREMERE OF DJ'S

MR. FLASHBACK

DJ DICE

FUNKING IT UP IN THE REGGAE, 70'S & HIP HOP CHAMBER!

MIKE MESSEX·DJ CHILL·DJ SHAGGY
RANKIN TOMAS & CULTURE D.

GIANT COMPUTERIZED ANIMATED VIDEO SCREENS BY
MIKE FILM GALAXY FX
MIND TWISTING PSYCHADELIC HALLUCINATIONS BY
AGE OF MACHINE LABORATORIES
RIOT ASS KICKING JBL BASS BY
((( SOUND BARRIER )))
ALSO FULL SPECTRUM MULTIPLE COLOR LAZER &
PSYCHADELIC LIGHTIING

rave giveaways & concessions by sjobeck & split

213-349-3636    310-281-5773    714-665-7799

# THEE L.A. RIOT AFTERMATH PAYBACK 1992
## FRIDAY JUNE 5TH

This will be a free payback for those of you who still have tickets from thee la riot on Sunday may 24th and for those who don't have tickets this event will only be $5. Also, we would like to apologize for the bust at midnight on may 24th as you know if you were one of the club goers that entered the builrding it was way over maximum capacity allowed so we were shut down by the officials. we'd just like to say we appreciate your understanding and support in the past And hope for your continued support in the future. Thank you

# PEACE!!!

THE LOST CITY OF
ATLANTIS
SAT.JULY 25, 1992 AD
marcelo92

Hawk and E-Clorexx brings you
# THE LOST CITY OF ATLANTIS...surfacing
# JULY 25TH 1992 A.D....an X-static E-vent
guaranteed to shake your shit! This E-vent will
take place in a virtual underwater playground.

**Atlantis** comes forth from the depths of the abyss to
overload your senses and submerge your minds in pure
Extasy. Your trip begins beneath the sea in the
**Chamber of Dementia** as your mind is engulfed by
strange, eerie **performance art**. Then the blacklit
abyss will unleash your frenzied desires as you pivot on
the floor of the ocean. Drawn by a heavenly groove, you
rise to the surface to find yourself in a **tropical
lagoon** surrounded by **waterfalls**, **mazes**, and
**caverns**. You **dance till dawn**, find your friends, and
it's off to Flammable!...

## DJ'S OF THE
## DEEP:
**RON D. CORE**
**SHAWN-PAUL**
**BARRY WEAVER**
**JUSTIN KING**
**JON WILLIAMS**
**VITAMIN D**
**JON BISHOP**
**DJ DAN** and live &
direct from England
**IAN CALLOWAY**

Call for info. & presale
ticket locations:

# 213.969.1845
# 310.280.3458
# 714.457.2122
# 818.377.5835
# 619.497.2026

LIVE PERFORMANCE BY **MOONPUP**
SPINNING HIS FAT TRIBAL BEATS
IN THE TROPICAL WONDERLAND..
...COMPUGRAPHX **SYNTHETRIX**
GO-GO's **K2**
SMART BAR **SMART MART**
CONCESSIONS **MISS KITTY'S**
DOPE RAGS **FAB THREADS**
CLOTHING **VERTIGO**
BODY ART **HOUSE PETS**
MIND E-X-PLORATION **X-PLORE**
**MINDE MACHINES**
SPINAL FLUID DISPLACEMENT
**MOONBOUNCE**
PAINTING **DIABOLICAL**
**BEATSWORTH**
CYBEROPTIC LOOPS **BRAD
BAKER**
SOUND **SHREDDER**
100% BUST FREE
**NO BULLSHIT**
EVENT!!
ALL PERMITS
SECURED



TRITON POWER

LEVIATHAN
SEPT • 5th

an event of enormous proportions
LEVIATHAN
SAT · SEPT · 5th
DJ'S BARRY WEAVER
MARKEM-X TONY LARGO
DJ DAN RON D. CORE
KANDYMAN DJ THEE ·O
SOUND · LIGHTING · INTELABEAMS
THE SHREDDER
LOOPS AND EFFECTS BY M&C GROOVY GO-GO'S
INFO
213·960·5572
310·281·1803
714·647·5532
C.B. DESIGNS/213·303·3876/WHO IS CHRIS GALVIN?

MONSTER MASH
HALLOWEEN
NIGHT

There is a hidden message on the front
of this scary mask. can you find it???

Beej Productions one of the 2 creative forces behind L.S.D. 1 & 2
S.E.X., Love, Nirvana, Babylon, Apococalypse, Saturnalia & Ahknaten
to name some spanning over the last three years Returns solo with a
complete new direction and attitude for the future of Los Angeles...

# MONSTER MASH

## halloween night  saturday oct 31st

Enter through our sacred gates of discordant doom, revel & compete in our costume contests hosted by moriah the batlady.the two categories are best horror & best fantasy. 2 grand prize winners will fly to London, England. 2 first place winners will fly to new york city. 2 second place winners will fly to san francisco & 2 third place winners will fly to las vegas. hard to believe? call continental airlines to confirm them at 800-525-0280 (under beej prod. costume prize winner). lose yourselves in our giant haunted mazes created by gary tesch of funhouse entertainment.

Free Cassette,
LP's & CD's
Courtesy of Sony / Epic

Giveaways include
Eon, Bizarre Inc
& Shamen

FREE! trick or treat with 1,000 lbs of free tasty treats & edible eats supplied by kitty koncessions passed out by rollerskating ghouls. dont be caught alone, for thru-out our event ghouls, goblins & monsters are looking to take your souls!!

your dispellers of hobgobling(hosts)include:
gary bizz • daven • tef • moriah • mike hiatus • tracey • chill & flick

### live performances by Moby & Lunatic Fringe

haunting house d.j.s
doc martin • robbie hardkiss
of San Francisco
chris flores • chris lum
mr koolaid • ron d core
danny zee • frankie
w/ shredders wall of doom
laser system and visuals by
n.y.s scott b

ghouly groove d.j.s
mike messex • sean perry
beej • riff raff
w/ boom boys 20 cabinet turbo drive
complete with authentic 60 x 60 ft
70s disco dancefloor w/ mirrorballs

Moby confirm Hotline 800.RAVELINE
Lunatic Fringe Hotline 213.243.9994

### Hollywood Park
### Racetrack & Pavillion
Price not to exceed $20

the backbone:mike h., lollpop,
natasha, tim, toni, gil & gary t.

213-243-2079   310-535-0893
714-239-9931   619-685-3683

call these lines now or endo
gets it in the face!!

PEYOTE
LOVE
BAZAAR
Saturday
September
26th

Saturday
September 26th
AGES PRODUCTIONS
Reach into yourself
Bring out your
innermost desires
and rejoice among
the spiritually
conscious
PEYOTE LOVE BAZAAR
Bazaar Bass by
THE SHREDDER
Trance Lights
& Lasers by
MIND OPTICS
DJ'S
STEVE LORIA
RON D CORE
ALDO BENDER
BARRY WEAVER
ELI STAR
CHRIS FLORES
LOVE LINES
213.707.0463
714.286.0972
310.355.4049

RIDING THE SUMMER OF LOVE
Truth
RAVING IN L.A.
100% PURE ENERGY

STEVE OF MOONSHINE    TEF OF LOST ANGELS
ARTIST GROOVE NETWORK
OF THE BOOGIE LOUNGE
GIVING YOU ALL AND NOTHING BUT
SATURDAY
SEPTEMBER 7TH
AT THE PARK PLAZA
607 S. PARK VIEW
10PM-4AM
ULTIMATE INTELLABEAM LIGHTWAVE
ORBS OF TRUTH BY XFX
THUNDER BASS BY COMBSOUND
TRIPLING YOUR PLEASURE
WITH TRIPLE THE MEASURE
MARK LEWIS
MICHAEL COOK
DOM T.
ROB HARRIS
OF THE BOOGIE LOUNGE
PLUS SPECIAL GUESTS
SELECTORMAN RAYSKI
AND ONCE AGAIN
URBAN DREAD
21 w/id
info: 213 550 1947
SECURITY PARKING AT WILSHIRE AND PARK VIEW . AVOID THE LINE— ARRIVE EARLY!
FIRST CLASS
US POSTAGE
PAID
LOS ANGELES CA
PERMIT NO 1240

SURPASSING ALL EXPECTATIONS
NOW EVEN MORE POWER
Truth
FEELING THE BRAVE
BUSTING OUT ON THE SCENE
JUST 1 SCOOP IS ALL IT TAKES

STEVE OF MOONSHINE IN ASSOCIATION WITH
MATT ROBINSON OF PEACE POSSE ● MR FRIENDLY ● ANDY LEHMAN & ROBY ROGERS OF BAD BOY PRODUCTIONS

THE SECOND CHAPTER

REGENERATED
RAVE
FOR THE FUTURE

TOTAL REALITY RETURNS

AT THE PARK PLAZA
607 S. PARK VIEW
LOS ANGELES

TRUTH

SATURDAY 10PM-4AM
MARCH 21ST

RAVE REGENERATION
TEKNO-ITALO-DEEP HOUSE GURUS

MARK LEWIS From London
DOMINATOR From Bristol
MICHAEL COOK From Manchester
JON WILLIAMS From London

CC AUDIO HOUSE SOUND
MIRAGE LAZERS
ULTIMATE INTELLABEAMS

FUNKAMENTALLY FRESH
FUNKY HIP HOP SOULFUL SELECTORS

MATT ROBINSON of Peace Posse
TOMAS of Flavor
JOHNNY of All 4 One
BOBBY B. of Bad Boys

140 DB+ FUNK SOUND
XFX ORBS OF TRUTH
MILKY WAY OPTIKINETIX

LIVE RASTA REVIVAL
RHYTHM TRAK POSSE

MOONSHINE DESIGN



FURTHER INFO: 310 550 1947
EARLY ARRIVAL DEFINITELY RECOMMENDED    21 W/ID    SECURE PARKING AT WILSHIRE & PARK VIEW

MOONSHINE EVENTS

SATURDAY
SEPTEMBER 5
SCREAMING YELLOW ZONKERS
92
ZONKING YOUR SOUL INTO
A NEW DIMENSION OF FUN

MIKIE, KAYA & TENORE OF
doobie funk productions
presents

SCREAMING
YELLOW ZONKERS
september 5, 1992

Tantalizing Your Taste for AmbientTechno:
DJ DAN  Ron D. Core
DJ's Thee-O  &  CandyMan

Funkin' It Up All NightLong
until the break of dawn
PIMP DADDIES:
Mike Messex & Sean Perry

Body Bouncing
Bass By: Shredder

Special Guest
FUNK & TECHNO
DJ's & ACTS
to be announced

Lights & Special
F/X: Brad Baker

Your Zonked Out Hosts: Dave' Capt-Kirk of climax
Moriah the Batlady & Brandon B#1 of Fresh Jive

FOR MORE INFO: (714) 720-8274 (213) 340-3780

TECHNOFLIGHT
MAY 30
AT THE SPRUCE GOOSE, LONG BEACH
A Gizmo Original

# TECHNOFLIGHT

AT THE SPRUCE GOOSE

Dy-na mix presents
the first L.A. appearances of +8 sound system
with special appearances of

## CYBERSONIK
## *F.U.S.E.*



With Guest D.J. RITCHIE HAWTIN
and L.A.'s very own DIMENSION 23

### Special FX
80,000 watts of pure concert sound
never before seen visual light extravaganza
bubbling dry ice swamp
strobe flowers
40 watt multi-color laser battles

## DEPARTING MAY 30th

### 213 281•9529
### 285•8574

## Pilots:
- JUSTIN KING
- DOC MARTIN
- MICHEAL COOK
- BARRY WEAVER
- DESTRUCTO

Taking you higher

**Additional Attractions:**
flourescent bubble machines • moonbounces
optikinetic projections • cyber-optic stimulations
full bar • snack bar • runway concessions

## TICKETS AVAILABLE AT

| COSTA MESA | | PASADENA | |
|---|---|---|---|
| NOISE, NOISE, NOISE | (714•556•6473) | POO BAH | (818•449•3359) |
| LONDON EXCHANGE | (714•650•1141) | **RESEDA** | |
| **FULLERTON** | 517 N. Harbor | CUTTING EDGE | (818•744•0710) |
| IPSO FACTO | (714•525•7865) | **RIVERSIDE** | |
| **HUNTINGTON BEACH** | | A PRIMARY | (714•276•9216) |
| VINAL SOLUTIONS | (714•963•1819) | **ROSEMEAD** | |
| **IRVINE** | | EXODUS RECORDS | (818•573•8818) |
| HYDE PARK CORNER | (714•838•0636) | **SAN CLEMENTE** | |
| **LONG BEACH** | | GATOR RECORDS | (714•361•3934) |
| TEN TON | (310•433•5484) | **SAN DIEGO** | |
| RECORD REACTION | (310•434•5753) | CATWALK | (619•696•9786) |
| **LOS ANGELES** | | **SANTA BARBERA** | |
| PRIME CUTS | (213•654•8251) | DEEP GROOVE | (805•963•6207) |
| D.M.C. | (213•651•3520) | **TORRANCE** | |
| STREET SOUNDS | (213•651•0630) | FUNKYTOWN | (310•373•0010) |
| FUNKEESENTIALS | (213•653•2585) | **VENICE** | |
| **ORANGE** | | STAR GROOVE | (310•314•2218) |
| ALLEY KAT | (714•633•6210) | | |
| **PACIFIC BEACH** | | | |
| AWE POSITION | (619•488•8832) | | |

**$20 PRESALE**
**$25 DAY OF EVENT**

AFTER BRINGING YOU COLOSSUS
THE CREATORS OF IN CONJUNCTION WITH
CHILI AND FLICK PRODUCTIONS PRESENT:
TNT
FRI. JULY 3. 92

CUSTOM PRINTING SERVICES 619.275.0293

TRUTH

STEVE OF MOONSHINE  TEF OF LOST ANGELS
ARTIST GROOVE NETWORK
OF THE BOOGIE LOUNGE
GIVING IT TO YOU HARDCORE
SATURDAY
AUGUST 10TH
10PM - 4AM
AT THE PARK PLAZA
607 S. PARK VIEW
TEN PACK SOUND BY CHRIS COMBS
ULTIMATE INTELLABEAM LIGHTING
SUSPENDED ORBS OF TRUTH BY XFX
ARTWHERE? BY JOEY KREBS LIVE
THREE RHYTHMS TO MOVE YOUR SOUL
IN THREE FULL ROOMS
housing yo' body
MARK LEWIS
MICHAEL COOK
DOM T.
funkin yo' mind
ROB HARRIS
OF THE BOOGIE LOUNGE
MIKE MESSEX
jammin' the rasta
SELECTORMAN RAYSKI
BACK BY POPULAR DEMAND
URBAN DREAD

Truth

FIRST CLASS
US POSTAGE
PAID
LOS ANGELES CA
PERMIT NO 1240

21 w/id
early arrival recommended
info: 213 550 1947
SECURITY PARKING
AT WILSHIRE AND PARK VIEW

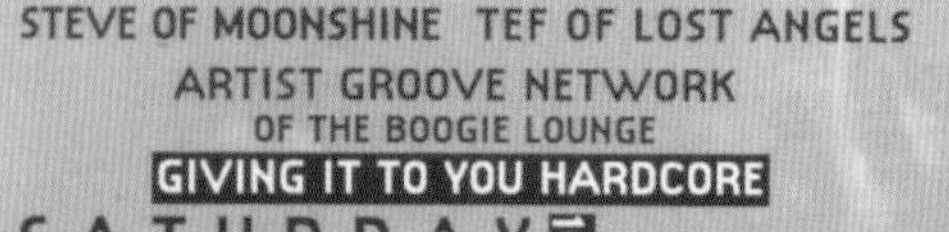

GLIMPSES OF TRUTH
design: moonshine & now you see it!!!
INFO:  310 550 1947
AT THE PARK PLAZA
607 S. PARK VIEW

POP N' FRESH
along with
matrix
PRESENT
DAVE GOODLEY
MISSY LA RUE
FUTURE PERFECT
AWAREHOUSE
OM LABORATORIES PROJECT 2
THE TECHNOLOGICAL TOTEM
CIRCA '93 PREVIEW
THANK YOU
BECAUSE OF YOUR OVERWHELMING RESPONSE TO THE MAGNITUDE OF THIS
MAJOR WORK IN PROGRESS AWAREHOUSE HAS BEEN MOVED TO
THE SHRINE EXPOSITION HALL

# A WAREHOUSE

## CIRCA '93 PREVIEW

11:00pm - 6:00am sunrise
do not arrive before 10:00pm

**saturday november**

## 21st
## 1992

the technological totem; a mobile interactive workstation encompassing both the physical (and the emotional science) and the emotional (religion, art, philosophy) in the creative matrix of the mind - center of perception. here is the perceptual revolution.

**djs**

**dat** digital audio technicians

**ignition:**

**sandra collins**
phoenix rising

**andre lucero**
santa barbara's finest

**system up·grade:**

**jon williams**
a real journey

**barry weaver**
techno turbo boost

direct from san francisco

**ernie munson**
electro love magnet

**download**

**jason bentley**
an introduction

**chris flores**
a journey completed

**live fast**
**dream hard**

NO PAY POINT buy presale or direct at the door DRIVE SAFE!!

$15 presale • $20 day of event

140 db+ — BoomBoy
introducing Mastersplinter

multi-9x12 Computer Screen
Video-Mix by OM & Victor

**m a n n i x : v i s u a l s**

**this is a second announcement see poster for much more!!**

**communications: info**

213 · 957 · 4943
818 · 418 · 2820
310 · 285 · 8404

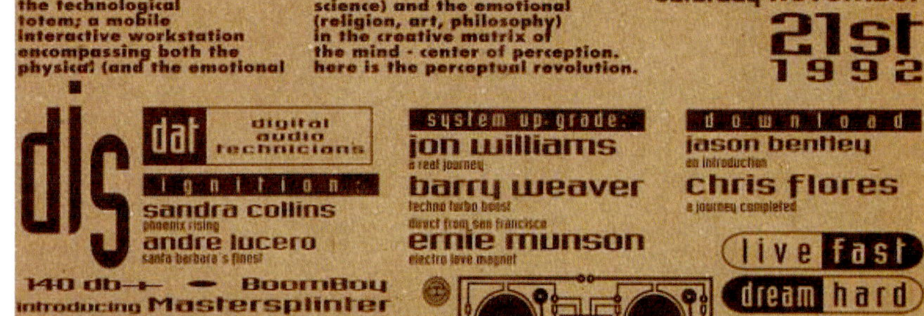

**TICKETMASTER**
MUSIC PLUS • MAY COMPANY • TOWER
213/480-3232 • (714) 740-2000

**ffn: all u** house freaks • garage lovers • techno gangsters • flatliners [ambient] • keep the faith

WONDERLAND
May 30th
A Tribe of Artists, DJs, and Ravers, sends your head on an Adventure
Alice Takes A Trip To The Land Where What Is Isn't

MAY 30 th 1992
A rave by the people for the people
WONDERLAND
Melts your mind when
Alice takes a trip
to the land where what is... isn't.
A vinyl explosion by
Steve Loria
Markem X
Ron D. Core
Chris Flores
[Back from the U.K.]
[Aerial - Paw Paw Patch]
Babylon
R.A.W.
(Double Hit Mickey)
(Shiva-No Doz)
Herbally Enhanced
Computer Projections
SAM I AM    M & C
Full Spinal Shocking
Bass by SHREDDER
Halucinogenic Props
& Psycho Eye Candy by
NOCTURNAL EMMISSIONS
Full Surround Laser
& Emulator Effects
ROD THE GOBSTOPPER
(Shiva-Raindance-Nitress)
Psychodelic Lighting
by NEPTUNE
Humpty Dumpty Bounce-
Smart Bar - Shaved Ice-
Free Toys- Free Candy-
by Mr. Do!
CWOBBER GWAPHICS
100% PURE SWEAT BOX WAREHOUSE
-PERMITS SECURED-
310-986-2778
INFO-YOUR-MATION
619-689-6178
$15
714-753-3336
$15

SATURDAY MAY 9th 1992 A.D.
THE MASTERS OF CEREMONY
WILLIAM KILL & JEZ
IN ALLIANCE WITH
DIGITAL NATION
COMES THE BATTLE OF
ARMAGEDDON
FEATURING LIVE ON STAGE
M O B Y
JOEY BELTRAM

deeper magic
from before
the dawn of time .
NARNIA
saturday July
18th

WILD KINGDOM
Saturday
September 26th

GREETINGS
OF THE 7 OPIUMS AND THIS SUMMERS 3000 PERSON FESTIVAL • NARNIA•
GLOBAL UNDERWORLD NETWORK
R.E.A.L.
PANDEMONIUM • ALTERN8 DIGITAL BOY • QUADROPHONIA FIERCE RULING DIVA
CHILI & FLICK
OF COLOSSUS
NATURALLY BRING YOU SO. CALIF'S LARGEST UNDERGROUND
ONE YEAR IN THE MAKING!
R.E.A.L EVENTS • GLOBAL UNDER WORLD AND CHILI & FLICK WANT TO OPEN THE CAGE TO
PURE • TRIBAL • TECHNO • HIP HOP LET YOUR MIND GO WILD MADNESS
TRIBAL TECHNO HUT
3 MASSIVE DANCE FLOORS WITH DJ's
HIP HOP JUNGLE
MARQUES WYATT
GREY BOY
DJ JAM
BEEJ
SEAN PERRY
STEVEN FLEX
ALYWAD
STEVE LORIA
MARK E. QUARK
BARRY WEAVER
DALE CHARLES
ALDO BENDER
JON BISHOP
ECSTATIC
FABIAN
B-SIDE
from san fran
ROBBIE HARDKISS
8 GIGANTIC CARNIVAL RIDES "ALL RIDES FREE"
GRAVITRON
SCRAMBLER
PARATROPPER
2 STORY FUNHOUSE
GIANT 40 PERSON SWING
BUNGIE JUMPING
7 STORY GIANT SLIDE
HOT AIR BALLOONS
ALL RIDES FREE W/ ADMISSION
9PM TILL 9AM
INFOVINES 213.243.9603 • 714.284.9517
619.685.3451 • 415.442.7690

# L.A. GROOVE
## PRODUCTIONS

Presents A Journey With The Master
Of Kaos & Disorder

# MXYZPTLK
(mix-yez-pittle-ick)

Invading the aura of you body and pushing
the barriers of your nuerol control.

**With Your
3-Dimensional
Wizards**

**BARRY WEAVER   MR. KOOL-AID
MARKEM X   BOY LONDON
RON D. CORE**

**Special apperences by:**

**DAZE • AFSHIN • MANN-E MARKOSH**

LASER
LIGHTS

Dimensional Emperors

ORBITRON
RIDE

**DAVEN THE MADHATTER**
(Paw Paw Patch)

MOON
BOUNCE

GIANT
PRISMS

**MIKE MESSEX**

Live Performance By:

**F.M.
CHEMICAL**

**RUSH**
(L.A. Groove Prod.)

and just added
live digital show by:
**DIMENSION 23**
(lead vocalist J-W-0-E.E.)

Eye Penetrating Laser Shows By:
**PSYCHO LASER & TALKING LASER CO.**

**Pulsating Bass By: BASS MOUNTAIN**

Retroactive 3-D
Computerized Video Screens
**MICHEAL FILM**

Full Blown Intellabeam
Light Show By:
**ELUMINATOR**

Consecions By:
Lords Of E. • Disiples • X-Static Hats
Miss Kitty's • Jiro Wear – Smart-Mart Bar

# Friday July 10th 92

(213) 869-5037 or 303-3542   (818) 505-2509

OUTPUT IS HELL!  © Hexa graffx 213 667 2200 / Mxyzptlk DC comics

6·20·92
NEMESIS
A REVOLUTION IS AT HAND
RE:design • N.Y.C. here we come!

saturday
6·20·92

némesis

A Revolution Is At Hand

Your Gods Of Fate
To Revolve Your Senses

chris flores
markem x
aldo bender
eli star

mr. buzz • cyrus • fester

strickly HUSH-HUSH
310.572.8283
this invitation intitles holder
to purchase 2 tickets

OmniCentre

# OmniCentre

Beginning **AUGUST 5TH**, from 12 PM-10 AM

A new weekly **Saturday Afterhours**
Brought to you by your friends
from **Magic Wednesdays**
Opening night featuring **Jonah Sharp**
and **Ernie Munson**

**10 Dollars**

| Omni Room | Geometric Jungle | Centrifugal Chill |
|---|---|---|
| DANIEL | JIMMY | BROCK |
| ELI STAR | FREDDY B | SYNTHETRIX |
| SANDRA COLLINS | JASON BENTLEY | HAREESH ONMARS |

Featuring Special Appearances by TAYLOR & SHAHEEN

A percentage of profits received from this event will go to the

**I.M.A.**
The Institute of Musical Art

AND

**P.E.M.A.**
The Foundation For The Preservation of Endangered Musical Art

HALO 44

6840 HOLLYWOOD BLVD.
(NEXT TO THE EL CAPITAN THEATRE)
CALL (310) 967-5080
FOR SPECIAL INFO ON GUESTS/DJs

WONDERLAND
Who Brought You
Alice Takes A Trip...
Sends Your Head
On Another
Journey
JULY
18th
RACER X
TURNS SPEED ON TO A NEW GROOVE
S&M

REVOLUTION

January 23, 1993
Saturday
Dj's
Barry Weaver
Steve Loria
Markem'X
Chris Flores
Mark Lewis
Sonic Bass & Blinding Lights by the SHREDDER
3 Rooms to dance your ass off!
TECHNO
HOUSE
CHILL OUT
Hip Hop Masters
BEEJ
"Big Daddy"
SEAN PERRY
info
310.217.7517
213.960.4342
818.377.4364
714.647.7775
Call these locations for special prices
pre-sale tickets
Fat Cat Burger · 310.541.0928
Exodus Records · 818.573.8818
Noise, Noise, Noise · 714.55.NOISE
Record Reaction · 310.434.5753
Italion Way · 310.316.5400
A&A Graphics & Printing 714.521.8784

TECHNOFLIGHT
AUG·8·1992
GIZMO ORIGINAL

TECHNOFLIGHT
AUG • 8 • 1992
GUERILLA RECORDS PRESENTS
U.K. RECORDING ARTISTS
REACT 2 RHYTHM
+
D.O.P.
TECHNOLOGICAL TURNTABLE MANIPULATION BY
JUSTIN KING • DOC MARTIN
BARRY WEAVER
FEATURING
THE RETURN OF THE COMPUTER CONTROLLED VARI-LIGHTS
100,000 WATTS OF PURE CONCERT SOUND
THREE DIMENSIONAL 40 WATT LASER LIGHT SHOW
OPTIKINETIC PROJECTIONS • CYBER-OPTIC STIMULATIONS
MOON BOUNCES • FULL BAR • SNACK BAR • CONCESSIONS
AND MUCH, MUCH MORE...AT AN ALL NEW LOCATION
310 • 281 • 9529
310 • 285 • 8574
G-GIZMO GRAPHICS (213)871-4055
PRESALE TICKETS AVAILABLE AT:
COSTA MESA
NOISE, NOISE,NOISE • 714-556-6473
FULLERTON
1950 FACTO • 714-525-7065
IRVINE
HYDE PARK CORNER 714-830-0636
LONG BEACH
TEN TON 310-433-5484
RECORD REACTION 310-434-5753
LOS ANGELES
PRIME CUTS • 213-651-0251
• D.M.C. 213-651-3539
STREET SOUNDS 213-651-0630
MONTEBELLO
SOUNDS OF MUSIC 213-721-0222
ORANGE
ALLEY KAT 714-633-6210
PACIFIC BEACH
AVE POSITION • 619-488-0832
PARAMOUNT
SOUNDS OF MUSIC 213-633-3727
PASADENA
POO BAH 818-449-3359
POMONA
STREETBEAT 714-469-6753
RESEDA
CUTTING EDGE 818-774-0710
RIVERSIDE
A PRIMARY 714-276-9716
ROSEMEAD
EXODUS RECORDS 818-573-0618
SAN BERNARDINO
JUXE 714-885-5180
GROOVE TUBE 714-884-0197
SAN CLEMENTE
GATOR RECORDS 714-361-3934
SAN DIEGO
CATWALK 619-484-9786
SAN FERNANDO
BEHIND THE GROOVE 818-361-8234
SANTA BARBARA
DEEP GROOVE 805-463-6207
THOUSAND OAKS
2MX 805-494-9395
TORRANCE
FUNKYTOWN 310-373-0010
$20 PRESALE

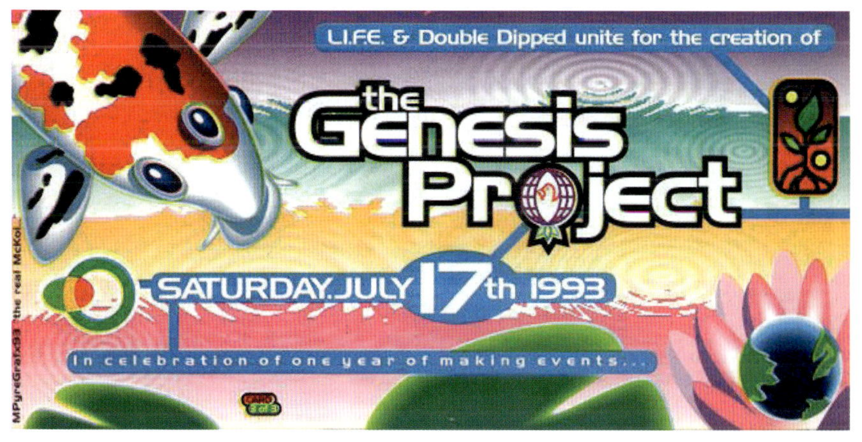

L.I.F.E. & Double Dipped unite for the creation of
the Genesis Project
SATURDAY. JULY 17th 1993
In celebration of one year of making events...
MPyreGrafx93   the real McKoi

L.I.F.E. & Double Dipped's One Year Anniversary
8 DJ's on Two Floors
15 Watt Multicolor and 12 Watt Argon Lazers from
Mirage
San Diego
Jon Bishop
Mark E. Quark
[after 4am]
Kaos-X
Los Angeles
Taylor
David Alvarado
And special guest from the UK
Jamie Cruisey
San Francisco
Simon
Bonz
Fun
Massive 48 Cabinet Sound System by
F.B.I.
Intelligent Lighting & Data Flash by
Equinox
Record Giveaways from Vinyl Frontier Music Distribution Network
"Spreading Unity Through Music"
619.685-2784   714.254-7332
213.955-1779   Emergency Line: 619.979-1097

brings you
TABULA RASA
18 & OVER
s a t u r d a y
JULY 11th
1 9 9 2
A percentage of proceeds will be donated
to the planetary transformation project

OKEE DOKEE GRAPE APE GRAPE APE!!
GIMME THAT OLD SCHOOL
ITEM $1